IN THE ATTACK OF OUTBACK JACK

D0112432

www.bigidea.com

Zonder**kidz**™

The children's group of Zondervan

www.zonderkidz.com

Larryboy in the Attack of Outback Jack
Copyright © 2003 by Big Idea Productions, Inc.

Requests for information should be addressed to:
Zonderkidz, Grand Rapids, Michigan 49530

ISBN: 0-310-70649-1

Written by: Doug Peterson
Editors: Cindy Kenney, Gwen Ellis
Cover and Interior Illustrations: Michael Moore
Cover Design and Art Direction: Big Idea Design
Interior Design: Big Idea Design and Holli Leegwater

CIP applied for
Printed in United States

05/RRD/5 4

BIG IDEA
BOOKS™

IN THE ATTACK OF OUTBACK JACK

WRITTEN BY
DOUG PETERSON

ILLUSTRATED BY
MICHAEL MOORE

BASED ON THE HIT VIDEO SERIES: LARRYBOY
CREATED BY PHIL VISCHER
SERIES ADAPTED BY TOM BANCROFT

Zonderkidz

TABLE OF CONTENTS

CHAPTER 1

THEY CAME FROM THE SEA

It started with screams.

Lots of screaming. Then the swimmers at Bumbly Bay Beach started running, scrambling for shore.

Was it a shark attack? A monster? A deranged beach ball? Mutant lifeguards running in slow motion?

No! It was worse. Much worse.

It was a kiwi fruit.

A crazed kiwi was driving his jeep right across Bumbly Bay like a motorboat. The amphibious jeep sliced through the water, scattering swimmers, and then roared out onto the beach, swerving wildly to avoid sunbathers.

Behind the wheel was none other than that dastardly driver, Outback Jack. And in the seat next to him was his evil sidekick, Jackie, who was busily reading a best-selling book, *The Doofus' Guide to Treasure Hunting*.

"Oy, love! We made it!" boomed Outback Jack, who was as much Australian as kangaroos and crocodiles. He wore a khaki shirt and bush hat and talked with the gleeful excitement of a little kid.

"G'day, Bumblyburg!" Outback Jack shouted, as the jeep veered onto a street. "Outback Jack's the name, and fortune hunting's me game!" Throwing his head back, he roared with laughter.

"Hmmmm—that's the last time I let you drive us across the ocean," said Outback Jack's evil sidekick from behind her book. "Look what it's done to my hair!"

She lowered her book, revealing the most sinister sidekick in the long history of sinister sidekicks. She was hideous. She was shocking. She was...

A sock puppet?

Yes, it's true. Outback Jack's sidekick was none other than Jackie, the Sock Puppet. But she wasn't just any old sock puppet plucked warm from the dryer. She looked like a crocodile with a pink pillbox hat.

Outback Jack had a very special relationship with the sock puppet perched on his right hand. He spoke to her, and she spoke back. (But truth be told, Outback did all of Jackie's talking for her, speaking in a very high-pitched voice.)

This kiwi had clearly spent too much time alone in the outback.

"We're going to be the richest blokes in the world once we steal the legendary Treasure of Bumblyburg," grinned Outback, as he made a sharp right turn and nearly ran over two gourds.

"We'll show 'em, Jack," said the puppet. "We're going to steal the treasure, and then we'll...**AHHHHHHHHHHHH!**"

The crocodile sock puppet stared straight ahead, open-mouthed with terror. The jeep was about to plow over Ma Mushroom. The little old lady had stepped off the curb and right into traffic, while casually licking her three-scoop ice cream cone.

SCREEEEEEEECHHH!

Outback Jack slammed on the brakes just in time. The jeep came to a skidding, squealing stop—inches before flattening Ma Mushroom.

Outback Jack couldn't help but stare at Ma Mushroom as the little old lady strolled in front of him, still licking her ice cream. In an excited whisper, he said, "Blimey! It's a flat-out Granny Crossing!"

Outback Jack crawled onto the hood of the jeep for a closer look. "Look how slow she moves," he gawked. "This is incredible! I've never seen a granny up close like this. They must be a very endangered species."

"Um...pardon us," Jackie the Sock Puppet crooned to Ma Mushroom in the sweetest tone. Then, in a voice that could shatter rock, she added, "*But could you please move it, sister!*"

Jackie's yell was so loud that the force lifted Ma Mushroom off her feet and blew her backward. Her ice cream cone flew out of her hand and landed on the head of a cucumber standing on the corner. As for Ma Mushroom, she landed upside down in a nearby trashcan.

"'At's tellin' the old toadstool, Jackie!" laughed Outback Jack. Then he put the jeep in gear and tore off, leaving the smell of burned rubber hanging in the air.

"Whippersnapper!" Ma Mushroom called after him from inside the can.

Meanwhile, the cucumber on whose head the cone had landed, paused to lick the ice cream streaming down his face. "My favorite flavor—vanilla cheese crunch!"

Yes, you guessed it! That cucumber was none other than Larry the Cucumber, and standing beside him was his trusted manservant, Archibald. (Larry calls him "Archie" for short.)

"I don't like the looks of this, Master Lawrence," said Archie.

"You're right. Vanilla cheese crunch stains easily," said Larry. "Do you think you can get it out of my shirt?"

"No, I mean that crazy kiwi," Archie clarified. "I think

he's up to no good."

"Oh, right. That too," Larry agreed as he tossed aside the ice cream cone. "This looks like a job for Larryboy!"

Larry whistled for a taxi, which came screeching to the curb. He flung open the door and leaped inside. With tires spinning like an Indy 500 racecar, the taxi sped ahead for...well...just about three feet. Then it came to another screeching halt, and the back door sprang open again.

Out leaped the caped cucumber. The defender of victimized vegetables. The purple, plunger-headed protector of...

"We get the point," urged Archie.

It was Larryboy!

"I AM THAT HERO!" Larryboy shouted as he hopped off in hot pursuit of Outback Jack.

CHAPTER 2

THE KING OF CHAOS

Wherever Outback Jack went, chaos followed, and pandemonium was about to descend on Bumblyburg.

Outback drove his jeep straight to the offices of the *Daily Bumble* newspaper—and I do mean *straight*. If there was a building in his path, he drove right through it, scattering shoppers, pulverizing mannequins, and wreaking havoc along the way.

As the crazy kiwi and his sock puppet pulled up to the newspaper building, Outback hopped onto his jet-powered, boomerang-shaped glider. Riding the boomerang like a flying skateboard, he soared right through the open window of Bob the Tomato's office on the top floor.

"WHAAAAA...?" said Bob, diving for cover.

With madcap glee, Outback Jack began to tear apart the offices of the *Daily Bumble* and made a monstrous mess as he hunted for information about the infamous Treasure of Bumblyburg.

"Hey! You can't do

that!" shouted Bob, the newspaper editor.

"Try to stop me, tomato-face!"

Rifling through Bob's file cabinet, Outback Jack flung papers in the air. Bob scurried around trying to catch them as they rained down upon his office.

But Larryboy was right behind him!

Our superhero had used his fruit-seeking radar to track the crazed kiwi right to Bob's office—although all he had to do was follow the trail of destruction. He raced through the door and skidded to a halt as he struck a heroic pose.

"Halt, you evil ice-cream-cone-wrecking, file-snatchers!" Larryboy announced.

"I'll handle this," whispered Jackie into Outback's ear. Then she turned toward Larryboy and batted her big, beautiful eyelashes. "My, my, but you're a *dashing* cucumber," she smiled coyly. "You know, I was just saying

to my friend Jack that toilet plungers are the one fashion accessory you don't see enough of these days."

Larryboy grinned at the compliment. "Oh...well, they're not only good looking, but they're practical as..." Larryboy paused and scowled. Pointing a plunger in Outback's direction, he proclaimed, "Flattery won't help you escape the long plunger of the law."

"Perhaps not, mate, but this will!" Outback said as he aimed Jackie at Larryboy's purple noggin.

You see, Jackie is more than Outback's silly sidekick sock puppet. She is also *The Power Glove of Doom!* Inside her pretty pink hat are some of the most deadly weapons known to veggies.

Outback pushed a button on the back of his puppet, and a tiny door popped open in the side of Jackie's hat.

Larryboy had no idea what was about to hit him.

CHAPTER 3

BEE-WARE!

A tiny bee flew out of the open door in Jackie the Sock Puppet's hat—flitting and flying and landing right on Larryboy's nose.

Larryboy stared at the bee, cross-eyed.

"Why, it's just a harmless little thing," he said.

"That's what you think, mate," chuckled Outback. "Larryboy, meet the Mega Jester-Bee!"

This odd little bee aimed its stinger directly at Larryboy's face and then fired a foul cloud of green gas. As the cloud of gas completely covered Larryboy's face, the superhero went stiff as a board. When the cloud vanished, Larryboy was wearing a pair of gag glasses—complete with black horn rims and a fake nose and moustache.

Even more terrifying, Larryboy launched into an uncontrollable, rapid-fire fit of joke-telling and laughter!

"What do polar bears eat for breakfast?" Larryboy asked. "Ice Krispies!

HAHAHAHAHAHAHA! What does a 2,000-pound mouse say to a cat? Here Kitty Kitty. HAHAHAHA-

HAHAHA! What did the French fry say to…?"

"Oh, now why'd you have to do that?" Jackie said to Outback. "He seemed harmless enough."

"Because we don't need some vigilante veggie spoiling our plan, luv," said Outback as he yanked out a file folder marked "Top Secret." "This file is going to give us a clue to the whereabouts of the Bumblyburg Treasure."

"What goes Ha-Ha-Ha-*Thump*?" Larryboy asked, barely able to control his giggling. "A person laughing his head off! **HAHAHAHAHAHAHA!**"

File in hand, Outback Jack hopped back onto his jet-powered, boomerang-shaped glider. Flames roared from its twin engines, and Outback shot out the window.

But no one else at the *Daily Bumble* was laughing… except for Larryboy, that is.

"What do you call a boomerang that doesn't come back?" he giggled as he cornered Bob the Tomato by the water-cooler. "A stick! **HAHAHAHAHAHA!**"

"Help," Bob squeaked.

But, twenty minutes later…

"What do you get when you cross a dinosaur with a pig?" Larryboy said, following Bob the Tomato around the newspaper offices. "Jurassic pork! **HAHAHAHAHAHA!**"

"The horror," winced Bob.

And still fifteen minutes later…

"How do you clean a tuba?" Larryboy asked as he chased Bob into the lunchroom. "With a tuba toothpaste! **HAHAHAHAHAHA!**"

"AHHHHHHHHHHHHH!" yelled Bob.

CHAPTER 4

A SNAKE IN THE FACE

While Larryboy continued to torment Bob with an endless string of bad jokes, Outback Jack continued his own reign of terror.

First, he flipped through the stolen file until he found the information he needed about the Treasure of Bumblyburg. Then he zoomed over to the Bumblyburg Clock Tower on his glider where he tied a rope to the clock face. Jackie latched onto the rope with her mouth and yanked at the clock with all of her might.

"Pull, Jackie! Pull!" shouted Outback.

Just as the clock was finally coming loose, a voice spoke from the roof of the Clock Tower: "Your time is up, Outback!"

Outback and Jackie exchanged startled looks as they gazed at the tip-top of the tower. There, with his cape flapping gallantly in the breeze, stood Larryboy.

"What 'appened?" Outback asked.

"Run out of jokes, Laffy-boy?"

"It's *Larryboy*!" the

caped cucumber corrected. "Your laughing gas wore off a little sooner than you planned—thanks to the forty cups of water that the Bumblyburg staff threw in my face. But now the joke's on you, Outback! Knock-knock."

"Who's there?" said Outback, unable to resist a good knock-knock joke.

"Alaska."

"Alaska who?"

"Alaska one more time: Give up or you're going to taste my plungers!"

"He's good," Jackie noted.

"But not good enough, luv!"

With that, Jackie and Outback gave a mighty heave-ho, and the clock face cracked loose from the wall. Torn free, the clock dangled mid-air, connected to Outback's glider by the sturdy rope.

Quick as a cat, Larryboy fired a plunger.

THONK!

The plunger stuck fast to the clock face. Now the tug-of-war began, with Outback pulling on one end of his rope and Larryboy yanking on the other end with his plunger.

Hovering just a few feet away, Outback thrust his sock puppet forward and once again, Jackie became *The Power Glove of Doom*.

This time, however, Larryboy was ready. A flyswatter popped out of Larryboy's superhero utility belt and whipped around like a fencing foil.

"My radar-guided flyswatter will take care of your Mega Jester-Bee, Outback Jack!"

"Yer blooming right, mate," said Outback. "But it'll only make me snake veeery mad."

"Snake?" Larryboy gulped. "Did you say snake?"

Larryboy's flyswatter wilted.

"Larryboy, meet my pet rattlesnake," Outback told him as the top of Jackie's hat burst open like a spring-loaded gag-box and a real snake launched forward.

The rattlesnake flew through the air in slow motion, jaws open wide, while Larryboy sprang into action. Pressing a button on his utility belt, he triggered a weapon specially designed to fight snakes.

BOING!

Out popped a cheese grater!

"Wrong weapon, wrong weapon," Larryboy grumbled. In a panic, he pushed another button. Out popped a set of measuring cups. Then an egg beater. A frying pan. Salt and pepper shakers.

"I'm beginning to get the feeling I put on the wrong utility belt this morning," Larryboy moaned.

So, with the snake only inches from his face, Larryboy did what any superhero would do in this situation.

He ran.

Outback Jack could barely stop laughing long enough to yell, "G'day, mate!" to the fleeing cucumber. Then he and his sidekick sock puppet flew off in the opposite direction, blazing across the sky, dragging the clock face close behind.

CHAPTER 5

GUMMYBOY!

Later that day...

"I thought for sure that I set out my Larryboy Ultra-Defender Utility Belt this morning," whispered Larryboy to the superhero in the seat beside him. "But I must have set out my Mother's-Little-Helper Kitchen Utility Belt by mistake. It was very embarrassing."

"SHHHHHHH," said the superhero next to him—a lemony hero known throughout the world as Lemon Twist.

Larryboy and Lemon Twist were just two of the students in a pretty extraordinary class—the Superheroes 101 Class at Bumblyburg Community College. The classroom was packed with superheroes of all shapes, sizes, and varieties. These were the amazing veggies and fruits that protected towns surrounding the entire Bumblyburg area.

"Tonight, as you know, we are going on a field trip to visit the original superheroes who once defended your towns," announced the class teacher, Bok Choy—a wise, old veggie. "We are going to visit the Bumblyburg Home for Retired Superheroes."

"Sounds like fun," whispered Larryboy to Lemon Twist. "I love field trips."

Lemon Twist tried to ignore him.

"Care for some Molar Madness?" Larryboy asked, leaning across the aisle. "It's bubblegum."

"SSSSSSHHHH," hissed Lemon Twist. "You know the rule—no gum or talking in class!"

Larryboy paused in the middle of a chew. "Oh, drat. I forgot. I better stash my gum until the end of class."

Scooping the huge wad of gum out of his mouth, Larryboy looked around for a good place to put it and finally decided that the safest place was on his utility belt. Little did he know that he'd placed the gum directly over the hole of his high-pressure air pump. A handy device if you have to pump up the tires of the Larrymobile.

"Please open your Superhero Handbook to Section 3, Paragraph 19, Line 32," Bok Choy instructed. "Perhaps Larryboy will read it for us."

"I'd be delighted," said Larryboy, picking up his Superhero Handbook. "Now, let's see, where's Section 3?" he added as he wildly flipped through his book.

Bok Choy cleared his throat. "It comes right after Section 2."

"Oh, right. I knew that," Larryboy grinned as he found the page. But in all of his moving about, he had accidentally bumped the trigger on the high-pressure air pump inside the back of his utility belt.

The bubblegum began to inflate. It grew bigger and bigger and bigger.

By the time Larryboy stood up, cleared his throat, and

began reading, "Rise in the presence of the aged. Show respect for the elderly and revere your God!" the bubblegum bubble on his belt had become the size of a basketball. But Bok Choy didn't notice because he had his back to the class as he wrote out the passage on the blackboard. Larryboy still hadn't noticed either.

But the rest of the class couldn't help but see.

There were a few snickers.

"So what does this passage mean, Larryboy?" asked Bok Choy, still scribbling on the blackboard.

"I think it means we should stand up whenever an elder superhero enters the room," Larryboy said, feeling quite pleased with himself. "Rising to your feet is a sign of respect and honor to those older and wiser."

And just as he spoke those very words, Larryboy began to rise—up in the air, his bubblegum bubble now the size of a large beach ball!

"That is correct, Larryboy," Bok Choy told him as he continued to write on the blackboard. "We can also show respect by opening doors for older people, helping them carry things, and listening to their words of wisdom. As superheroes, your elders have a wealth of knowledge and experience from which you can learn. Listen to their stories and you, too, can gain insights from their wisdom."

"How did I get up here?" Larryboy asked as he floated toward the ceiling.

"How do we revere?" Bok Choy asked, not quite clear on what Larryboy had said. "To revere your God means we are called to worship and respect him. God is all-knowing. We can trust and learn from his word, more than any other."

Bok Choy finally turned to face the class and added, "Now tell me, what else can we...?" He stopped mid-sentence and stared. Larryboy was gone. He wasn't in his seat. And he wasn't standing next to his desk.

Bok Choy's eyes drifted to the ceiling where Larryboy was floating up, up, up!

"I don't think this is what the passage meant by rising in the presence of your elders," noted Bok Choy, dryly.

At that very moment, the giant bubblegum bubble on the back of Larryboy's utility belt touched the fluorescent light on the ceiling.

POP!
CLUNK!

Larryboy dropped to the floor like a rock, completely covered with the popped bubblegum.

Larryboy sucked some of the gum back into his mouth, smacked his lips, and grinned. "Mmmmm, they're right! It's juicy and refreshing and leaves your breath minty fresh."

"Class dismissed," sighed Bok Choy.

The superheroes left the room, anxiously talking about their field trip to the Bumblyburg Home for Retired Superheroes. Unfortunately, Larryboy had to *stick* around a little longer than he had planned. After all, they didn't call it Molar Madness for nothing!

Little did Larryboy know that his sticky situations were just beginning.

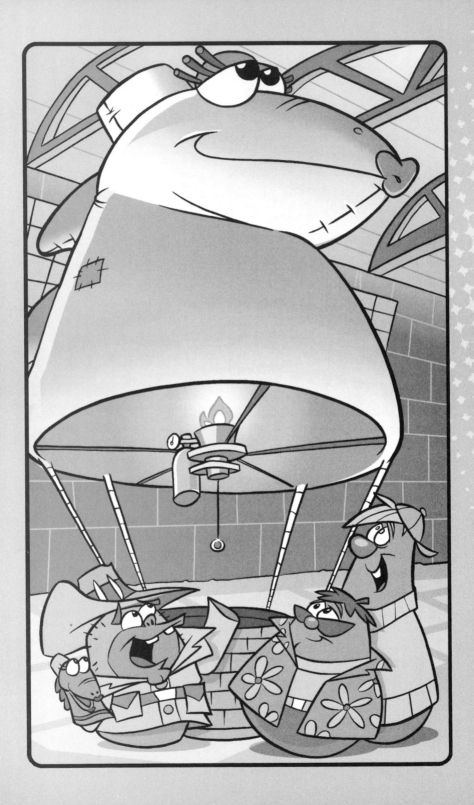

CHAPTER 6

THE BALLOON BANDITS

It was time for the superheroes to take their field trip to the Bumblyburg Home for Retired Superheroes. But as the superheroes headed for the Home, time did not stand still for the dastardly doings of Outback Jack.

After stealing the clock, Outback landed his glider inside the gates of the famed Bumblyburg Balloon Factory—the greatest balloon factory in the world. The factory made everything from giant hot-air balloons to various types of balloon animals.

"It's a beauty!" said Outback Jack, staring up at a hot-air balloon that had been built on the main factory floor. The factory owners, Herbert and Wally, had taken him there to show off the balloon he'd ordered months before.

"Isn't she fantastic?" Outback asked Jackie the Sock Puppet.

Jackie was stunned. She didn't know what to say. "It *is* gorgeous! It's…it's…it's *me!*"

Jackie was right. The giant, hot-air balloon was built to look exactly like her—a giant crocodile sock puppet with a pretty pink hat.

"I'm glad you like it," said Herbert. "We have your bill all ready for you."

"And then the balloon will be yours," added Wally.

"Well...I've been meaning to talk to you blokes about that," said Outback, still staring wide-eyed at the hot-air balloon. "You see, mates, I don't have any money to give you."

Herbert and Wally exchanged glances. "No money? Then I'm afraid you can't have the balloon, Mr. Outback."

Outback finally made eye contact with the two potatoes. He had a sly smile. "I pay in different ways, mates. I have a little something socked away for times like this."

Snickering, Outback aimed his sock puppet right at Herbert and Wally. Then he pushed a button on The Power Glove of Doom.

CHAPTER 7
PRUNEMAN

Meanwhile,
Bok Choy's superhero class
piled into a school bus and drove to the
Bumblyburg Home for Retired Superheroes
on the east side of town. It was their first
field trip since the time they toured a super-
herocape factory in Puggslyville.

The retirement home was a bright, energy-
packed place. Elderly superheroes tested their old
superpowers by climbing on ceilings and walls,
while others traded stories and exchanged laughs.
There were numerous signs posted for all kinds of
amazing activities:

"HOW TO USE YOUR DENTURES TO FIGHT OFF MUTANTS."
"ROCKET-POWERED WALKERS: THE WAVE OF THE FUTURE"
"TEST YOUR X-RAY VISION AT THE WEEKLY HEALTH SCREENING."

Moving past rooms along a hallway, Bok Choy
and Larryboy spotted a large grapefruit superhero
sitting in a beach chair inside a kiddie pool. The
grapefruit calmly read the morning paper, while

gentle arches of water spouted from his head and back like a fountain.

"Hey, it's the Incredible Leaking Man!" Larryboy whispered, peeking his head into the room. "I thought he ran out of juice years ago."

"Old superheroes have more juice left in them than you think." Bok Choy divulged as he ushered Larryboy into the multi-purpose room. "Larryboy, may I present Pruneman, Bumblyburg's very first superhero."

Pruneman was...well, a prune—a little wrinkly and very old. He wore a green cape and had a large picture of a prune on his chest in bold colors. But what stood out the most were the two enormous ears attached to his mask.

Pruneman's eyes lit up at the sight of Bok Choy. "Bok Choy, you old stunt-monkey, you! How long's it been, partner?"

"Too long, my friend," said Bok Choy, as the two friends bowed to each other.

"Hey, remember that Invisible Ninja Flip you taught me?" said Pruneman, giving Bok Choy a nudge. "I can still do it after all these years!"

With those words, Pruneman went through a series of "Crouching Prune, Hidden Dragon" moves. A back flip. A tornado spin. A quick sprint up the wall. Finally, with one big burst of energy, Pruneman did a double back flip, then sprang right through the nearest door—and vanished.

Impressed, Larryboy and Bok Choy hurried through the door after him. But Pruneman was nowhere to be seen.

"WOW!" Larryboy said. "He completely disappeared!"

"Ahem," came a voice from above. "I didn't exactly disappear."

Larryboy and Bok Choy glanced upward. Pruneman was tangled in the chandelier.

"I've leaped, and I can't get down!" said Pruneman, wincing. "Oh, that's going to hurt in the morning. Ouch! Come to think of it, that hurts now."

CHAPTER 8
THAT'S THE PITS

Larryboy couldn't believe that Pruneman had once been Bumblyburg's number-one superhero. Why, the guy couldn't even do a simple ninja move without needing to speed-dial 911! Every student from Bok Choy's class had been paired up with a senior superhero, and Larryboy had been assigned *Pruneman*. Bok Choy said it was a great honor to have Bumblyburg's oldest superhero for a partner. But Larryboy couldn't see why. He was bored.

When Bok Choy found Larryboy, the caped cucumber was moping around by himself at the refreshment table. While, Pruneman was on the other side of the room—standing alone in front of an oscillating fan watching his cape billow in the breeze.

"Larryboy, haven't you been talking with Pruneman?" Bok Choy inquired.

"About what? The guy's a dinosaur."

"Most people think dinosaurs are pretty fascinating creatures," Bok Choy pointed out.

"You know what I mean," Larryboy said. "The only thing we have in common is that we both look good in a cape!"

At that very moment, Pruneman edged a little too close to the fan. Suddenly, the fan's blade yanked the old guy's cape with a ferocious tug and in a matter of seconds, the fan had totally shredded it up, leaving Pruneman completely capeless.

"Okay," Larryboy sighed, "now we have nothing in common," he said.

RIIINNNGGGGG! RIINNNNGGGG!

"Excuse me, Bok Choy, but my ears are ringing," Larryboy said.

It was Larryboy's Plunger-Com—a secret radio hidden inside Larryboy's plungers.

"Come in, Larryboy!" Archie's voice squeaked.

"I'm here," Larryboy told him. "What's happening, Archie?"

While Larryboy answered the call, Pruneman snatched the checkered tablecloth off the refreshment table, whipping it around his neck and turning it into his new cape. Then he moved in closer, trying to hear what Archie had to say.

"Something very strange is going on at the Bumblyburg Balloon Factory," Archie said.

"The Balloon Factory?"

"Yes. There are reports that the night shift has broken out with a serious case of bad jokes."

"That sounds like the work of Outback Jack! I'm on my way, Archie."

"Lemme help, Larryboy," pleaded Pruneman as he came up from behind him. "I can still use my famous Prune-Pit-Power-Up Move!"

"Your what?"

"My Prune–Pit–Power–Up Move! Just watch. You'll be quite impressed."

With a look of sheer determination, Pruneman began to fire prune pits—big, fat seeds—out of the large ears built into his superhero mask.

RAT-A-TAT-A-TAT-A-TAT-A-TAT!

Like a machine gun, the prune pits came out in rapid-fire fashion. But Pruneman had one little problem. His head was out of control, bouncing around like a bobble-head doll, firing prune pits in all directions.

"Hey watch it!" shouted two elderly superheroes, ducking underneath the folding table where they were playing checkers.

"I guess I'm a little rusty," Pruneman said, smiling awkwardly. He was feeling a bit wobbly after the prune pits finally stopped firing. "But I can still help you battle this Outback Jack character!"

Larryboy rolled his eyes as he helped Pruneman into a nearby chair. "Sorry, old fellow. But this is a job for some-one...well, someone with a little more speed and strength. Some other time, Pruneman."

As Larryboy sprinted out of the room, Pruneman watched him go with a twinge of sadness. He remembered the old days, when he had once been faster than a speeding water-melon seed...more powerful than a pumped-up papaya...able to leap tall celery in a single bound.

It didn't seem so long ago...

"Hey, Larryb—**WHHOAAAAA!**" Pruneman called out.

RAT-A-TAT-A-TAT-A-TAT-A-TAT-A-TAT!

The old guy's ears suddenly started firing prune pits again. The barrage made his chair spin like a pinwheel firework—around and around and around.

"Cut it out, Pruney!" shouted the nearby superheroes, as they ducked under their table once again.

"Ouch!"

"Incoming!"

Bok Choy looked on and sighed. Pruneman was in no shape for the perils that lay ahead.

CHAPTER 9

A STICKY SITUATION

The jokes were flying fast and furious at the Bumblyburg Balloon Factory.

"Why did the gum cross the road?"

"Because it was stuck to the chicken's foot."

"Why don't people play games in the jungle?"

"Too many cheetahs."

"What goes up and doesn't come down?"

"Your age."

HaHAHaHaHaHAHaHAHaHAHaHaHAHaHaHA!

The balloon factory workers rolled on the ground, holding their sides and howling with laughter. They could do nothing to stop Outback Jack, who busily connected his jeep to the bottom of the giant hot-air balloon. Mounted to the front hood of the jeep was the clock face he had ripped from the Bumblyburg Clock Tower.

Meanwhile, Larryboy was on his way to the factory in his Larryplane—a gadget-filled wonder created by his butler, Archie. In the darkness of evening, the plane hovered directly over the main factory building.

"Archie, is this the right place?" Larryboy asked over his Larryplane radio.

"Yes, I believe it is," said Archie. "My sensors are picking up a lot of laughter inside the building."

"Roger that," agreed Larryboy as he pushed a button on his instrument panel. The bottom of the Larryplane opened up to reveal rows and rows of plungers. With another push of the button, dozens of plungers rained down from the Larryplane and gripped the factory roof.

THWACK! THWACK! THWACK! THWACK!

By reeling the plungers back up toward the plane, Larryboy literally peeled off the metal roof of the factory like a pop-can tab. As he suspected, Outback was hiding inside the building, getting ready to launch his huge hot-air balloon.

"Outback, prepare to feel the sting of my plungers!" shouted Larryboy.

"Oy, mate! I'm shaking in me boots. I hate to say it, pickle boy, but you're filled with more hot air than this heeeere balloon."

Just then, a taxi came screeching up to the front door of the balloon factory. The door was thrown open—twice. (The first time, the door bounced back and closed before anyone could get out.) Eventually, Pruneman leaped out and told the taxi driver, "Keep the meter running. This won't take long." Then Pruneman hurdled forward, paused to strike a heroic pose, and ran to the factory building's front door.

Grabbing a fistful of balloons used to decorate each side of the front entrance, Pruneman quickly rose into the air. When he reached the top of the factory building, he let go of the balloons and leaped onto the roof. Even with a checkered tablecloth for a cape, Pruneman looked pretty impressive standing on top of the building, staring up at the Larryplane.

"Don't worry, Larryboy!" he shouted. "The Pit Crew has arrived!"

Larryboy groaned. This is no good. What can an old guy like Pruneman do to help?

To make matters worse, Larryboy realized he had something else to groan about—gum in the cockpit. Archie had always told him never to chew gum on a superhero mission. But he couldn't resist chewing a huge wad of Molar Madness. He also couldn't resist playing with his gum. As a result, a string of gum now connected his nose to the Larryplane controls, completely gumming up the cockpit.

Just then, Outback fired up his giant hot-air balloon and the massive ship slowly rose into the air. The expanding balloon was so huge that it barely fit through the open roof.

"Uh-oh," gulped Pruneman.

Uh-oh was right. Pruneman was standing on a narrow edge of the roof. If he wasn't careful, the balloon would bump him right off!

Outback steered the craft slightly to the right, and the giant crocodile balloon gave the ancient superhero a gentle nudge. That was all it took.

Pruneman teetered on the edge of the roof, trying to regain his balance. But all he could do was hope there'd be someone down below to catch him.

"Enjoy your fall Down Under," Outback Jack laughed.

Pruneman screamed, "*Larryboy!*" before he fell backward off the roof.

Pruneman plummeted toward the ground.

CHAPTER 10

IT GETS EVEN STICKIER

Pruneman was forty feet from the ground and falling fast.

Larryboy had to act quickly. But that was easier said than done. His string of gum had now turned into five strings of sticky stuff, creating a bubblegum web inside the cockpit.

The caped cucumber pressed the Larryplane joystick, and the plane dove down toward the falling prune. But Larryboy was so busy untangling himself from the gum that he nearly drove the Larryplane right into the side of the balloon factory.

Pruneman was thirty feet from the ground.

There were now ten strings of sticky gum connecting the controls to Larryboy's face.

"Plungers away!"

Larryboy managed to fire two plungers at Pruneman, but having to shoot through the maze of gum, one of them hit the side of the building and stuck. Still connected to the plunger's tether line, it caused the plane to whip around the building like a carnival ride.

Pruneman was twenty-one feet, four and one half inches from the ground.

Larryboy had only one hope left—a heat-seeking plunger that Archie had just invented. It had never been used before.

Pruneman was thirteen feet from the ground.

"That's roughly four meters in metric measurements!" Pruneman yelled as he fell.

POW! ZIP!

The heat-seeking plunger tore through the tangle of gum and streaked across the sky.

Pruneman was only three feet from the ground.

THWACK!

The heat-seeking plunger hit Pruneman smack in the middle of his back and stopped his fall just in time.

"Nice gadget," Pruneman noted, as he dangled just two inches from the cement. "We've got a toilet backing up in the lounge you might want to look at."

Although he was pleased he had saved the old super-hero, Larryboy was frustrated beyond belief. Outback Jack and his Balloon of Doom had vanished into the dark night, and Larryboy was in no shape to pursue him. Twenty-five strings of gum now crisscrossed the cockpit, and even more gum decorated the upholstery.

Larryboy had just enough gum left to blow a bubble, but it popped in his face.

"Drat."

CHAPTER 11

CLUES AND CONNECTIONS

The next morning at the *Daily Bumble* newspaper, Bob the Tomato called an urgent meeting. Vicki, the staff's top photographer, was there, along with cub reporter, Junior Asparagus. Larry the Janitor was mopping the floor...

...and listening.

Little did they know that mild-mannered Larry the Janitor was really Larryboy! You see, Larryboy was the only superhero with two secret identities. Sometimes he was Lawrence, the fantastically rich, courteous cucumber; and other times, he was Larry the Janitor.

"Outback Jack stole my research file on the town's founding fathers," Bob explained to his staff as he paced the floor.

"And then he stole the town clock," said Vicki.

"And he stole a giant hot-air balloon," added Junior.

"What's the connection?" asked Bob.

"I know!" shouted Larry the Janitor, wheeling around to face Bob and accidentally knocking Junior out of his seat with his mop handle. "They all have to do with *saving*!"

"Saving?" asked Vicki.

"Yes!" Larry shouted, wheeling around to face his favorite photographer. But as he gazed into Vicki's attractive eyes, he accidentally smacked Bob out of his seat with the mop handle. "You 'save' things in a research file."

"Yeah, but what about the clock?" Junior reminded him.

"A clock tells time! And you can 'save' time," Larry exclaimed. He wheeled around to face Junior and nearly swept Vicki off her chair with his mop handle. She ducked just in time.

"Then what about the hot-air balloon?" asked Vicki. "What does it have to do with 'saving'?"

Larry paused and stared blankly at Vicki. "Well...er...a hot-air balloon contains...um...air...and air is something that planes fly through...and...um...when a plane turns right, it is called 'banking' to the right. And a bank is where you keep money that you...um...'save.'" Larry smiled weakly.

"You don't really know how the balloon connects to the other things, do you?" asked Bob.

"Not a clue."

Suddenly, Larryboy's mop began to beep. Bob, Vicki, and Junior blinked in surprise.

"Your mop is beeping," Junior pointed out.

"Uh...yes," said Larry, staring awkwardly at his chirping mop. "My...uh...my automatic spill detector has automatically detected a spill. Gotta go!"

Larry the Janitor dashed out of the room, scurried into the janitor closet, and plopped the string mop over his head. Dirty water dripped down his face. He made a note to squeeze the water out of the mop *before* covering his head with his radio mop the next time.

"Hello, Master Lawrence." Archie's voice came through a screen that illuminated under the mop. The flickering image was of the asparagus butler standing in front of a panel of computerized equipment. "Bok Choy called to remind you to finish your superhero class assignment."

"Aw, but Archie," whined Larry. "I hate spending time with Pruneman. He's so out of touch. Pruneman messed up everything yesterday. If he hadn't tried to help, Outback never would have gotten away."

"May I remind you about the gum?"

"Point taken. But Pruneman is so *old*. Can't you tell Bok Choy I'm too busy to go to the retirement home?"

"After the bubblegum incident in class yesterday, he said your grade depends on this," said Archie.

"I'll be there in ten minutes."

Twenty minutes later, Larryboy was back in the halls of the Bumblyburg Home for Retired Superheroes. He paused in front of a sign that said, "Today: Superhero Bingo."

"Hey, maybe this won't be so bad after all," Larryboy said to himself. "After all, I like Bingo."

Larryboy pushed open the door to the multi-purpose room, expecting a calm game of Bingo with the old folks. Just a nice, easy-going, quiet...

POW! KA-BLOOEY! SWOOSH! BA-BOOM! RAT-A-TAT!

Entering the room, Larryboy was greeted by an explosion
of noise. Superhero weapons were firing from every corner.

CHAPTER 12

LASERS AND LIGHTNING AND LINT, OH MY!

Lasers streaked across the multi-purpose room. So did lightning bolts, streams of extra-hot taco sauce, snowballs, grappling hooks, bungee cords, sock lint, harpoons, and ping-pong balls.

Diving for cover, Larryboy made his way underneath the walkers, chairs, and tables, while deadly objects flew through the air right above him. It was like being in a war zone. Larryboy eventually squirmed his way to where Pruneman was sitting.

"Larryboy!" Pruneman shouted happily, looking down at his purple friend. "What a surprise! Wanna play Superhero Bingo with me!"

"This is Bingo?" Larryboy asked, crawling up and onto a chair. The weapons had finally stopped firing. "I thought Bingo was…uh…a quieter game."

"Not with superheroes," chuckled Pruneman. "See those giant Bingo cards over there by the wall?"

Larryboy nodded. On the far wall was a line of enormous Bingo cards. The cards were splattered, charred, and stuck with just about every superhero weapon imaginable—from mud-bombs and ice cream to darts and fireballs.

"My card is the third one from the left," said Pruneman. "If they call a number that's on my card, I fire my prune pits at it. I have to hit just the right spot on the card for it to count," Pruneman giggled. "Unfortunately, a lot of us don't have the aim we used to have."

So true. Most of the shots were way off the mark. A lot of the superhero weapons misfired and missed the target altogether, doing deep damage to the wall behind the cards. In fact, an entire section of the multi-purpose room's wall was missing.

"B-4," said a voice over the intercom.

"That's me!" shouted Pruneman, jumping out of his chair.

Weapons fired from all sides.

POW! KA-BLOOEY! SWOOSH! BA-BOOM! RAT-A-TAT! CLICK, CLICK, CLICK.

Pruneman tried to fire prune seeds from his ear, but nothing came out.

"Aw fiddlepits!" he said. "I've got B-4, but I'm fresh out of pit power." Pruneman turned to Larryboy. "Quick, fire a plunger for me at B-4."

"Huh?"

"Fire a plunger at B-4 on my Bingo card! If I win this game, I'll get an all-expense paid trip to Flimflamhamshire for the annual polyester harvest!"

Larryboy stood up and stared at the Bingo card—like a gunslinger sizing up his enemy. His eyes narrowed as he took aim.

FWAPPPP!

Larryboy's plunger zipped across the room, threading its way through the barrage of weapons.

THWACK!

The plunger hit dead center on B-4.

"Hot diggity!" Pruneman shouted, jumping into the air. "Larryboy, you're a natural at this game!"

"Nice shot, young fellow!" said an elderly superhero carrot from his rocking chair—which hovered in mid-air.

"That's my partner," said Pruneman proudly. He smiled at Larryboy.

As a couple of other senior superheroes nodded their approval, a smile grew on Larryboy's face. He was actually beginning to like this.

Even more surprising, he was beginning to like Pruneman.

CHAPTER 13

A BLAST FROM THE PAST

Later that day, Larryboy
rose from his chair as Pruneman
strolled into the room, carrying a photo
album.

What an afternoon it had been. After three
rip-roaring games of Superhero Bingo, Larryboy
and Pruneman spent the rest of the afternoon
scaling walls and trying out a new supercharged
wheelchair. It was the only wheelchair in the world
with a jet engine, helicopter blades, a smoke screen,
and a laser-guided Slushie-tossing slingshot.

Larryboy didn't know that an old guy could be so
much fun.

When the afternoon of action was over, Pruneman
invited Larryboy to the retirement home's Clock Room
for a glass of iced tea—and a peek at an old photo
album.

"This Clock Room is an amazing place," Larryboy
said, glancing around at the hundreds of clocks
lining every wall. There were grandfather clocks,
water clocks, cuckoo clocks, and an entire
shelf-load of hourglasses filled with sand.

"The fellow who built our retirement home was really fascinated by time," Pruneman noted. "Maybe that's why he was so interested in us old folks. We've all seen a lot of time go by."

Pruneman opened up the photo album and spread it out on a coffee table. "Speaking of time, here's the photo I wanted to show you. It's from a long time ago."

The black and white photo showed a much younger Pruneman blasting a volley of prune pits at a supervillain perched high atop the Clock Tower.

"WOW!" exclaimed Larryboy. "Is that you fighting the Evil Squashinator?"

"Sure is."

"I heard all about the Squashinator—a giant robotic squash that had been programmed to squash all the buildings in Bumblyburg by sitting on them. Was it you who defeated the Squashinator?"

Pruneman blushed. "Yes, it was. But that's not why I wanted to show you this photo."

Larryboy's eyes lit up. Who would have thought that an old guy like Pruneman had once been a young hero capable of defeating the Squashinator? Why, if it hadn't been for Pruneman, Bumblyburg wouldn't even exist today!

"I wanted to show you this photo because it might shed some light on what Outback Jack is up to."

"Really?"

"Maybe. You said that Outback Jack stole a file and then he stole the town clock, right?"

Larryboy nodded, eager for Pruneman to go on.

"Well, there's an old legend that the town clock originally belonged to Sir Lester Bumbly and Sir Mortimer Burg."

"Bumblyburg's founding fathers!" Larryboy gasped. "Bob was going to do an article about them before Outback stole his research file."

"Legend has it that they hid their family fortune to keep it away from attacking pirates. There's even a story that says they painted a secret map to the treasure on the face of the town clock."

Pruneman held a magnifying glass over the photo of the Clock Tower, while Larryboy took a close look. On the clock face were lots of fancy pictures surrounding the numbers. At the very top, above the number twelve, was a drawing of three hills—with a rock structure built upon the one in the middle. A stream of sunlight passed straight through a hole in the center of it.

"Those are the three hills on the edge of Bumblyburg," Larryboy said, whistling. "And I recognize that rock structure—it's the Rock of Time. Do you think this is the treasure map?"

Pruneman nodded solemnly.

"But how do you know all this?"

"You live. You listen. You learn," Pruneman explained, solemnly.

Larryboy stood up straight and looked very heroic. "Well, if Outback Jack is using that clock map to steal the Treasure of Bumblyburg, then it's my job to foil his evil plan!"

As Larryboy made a move to leap through the nearest window, Pruneman tried to stop him. "But wait, Larryboy! There's one other important thing you need to know!"

"No time for that, Pruneman! I AM THAT HERO!"

"But Larryboy...You need to know..."

Too late. Larryboy was already out the window and leaping into his Larrymobile. Time does not wait for a superhero on the move.

CHAPTER 14

WHALLOPING WALLABEES!

Evening crept across the city of Bumblyburg. But despite the darkening hours, Bumbly Park in the center of town was still packed with veggies. Some were walking their dogs. Others were taking their daily jog. And a number of elderly veggies were playing chess.

Above them, an ominous shadow drifted across the park like an evil cloud. It was the shadow of a hot-air balloon floating across the sky. Most veggies thought it was a strange sight on this clear, beautiful evening. And there was one very odd thing about the balloon—instead of a basket, a jeep was connected to its bottom.

Little did they know…

Outback rode through the air in his floating jeep, staring off into the distance toward three hills. On top of the middle hill was the famous rock structure, the Rock of Time.

"There they are, luv," he told his sock puppet. "The three hills.

And unless I'm mistaken, we'll find out where the treasure is buried right about *now*."

As the sun dipped behind the hills, it moved into just the right spot for a beam of sunlight to shoot through the hole in the center of the Rock of Time. Like a golden laser, the sunlight beam shot straight down from the hillside and struck the statue of Sir Lester Bumbly, located in the very center of the park.

"Blimey," said Outback, his eyes glittering. "The beam points right to the spot where the treasure is hidden. It must be buried beneath the statue."

"We're going to be rich!" Jackie shrieked.

"Time to start diggin'," said Outback. "But first, we need to clear the park, luv."

Raising a megaphone to his mouth, Outback leaned over the edge of his jeep. "Citizens of Bumblyburg," he called to the veggies far below. "Go home. Get out of the park...*now*!"

The veggies looked at each other in confusion. Several dogs barked at the hot-air balloon. Ma Mushroom stared up and yelled, "Whippersnapper!"

"Why should we leave the park just because you say

so?" said a middle-aged carrot.

"Who do you think you are?" shouted a pea.

"We're in the middle of a chess game!" yelled an elderly asparagus.

Outback Jack sighed and looked his sock puppet in the eyes. "Well, Jackie, we can't say we didn't warn them."

"If you don't leave *now*, I'll be forced to release me outback wall-a-bees," Outback Jack warned them.

But no one appeared frightened.

"Wallabies? Aren't they cute little kangaroos?" asked Herbert who was having lunch in the park with Wally.

"I think so. I'm not afraid of a wallaby," answered Wally.

"I warned ya!" shouted Outback Jack. "Here's me wall-a-bees!"

Jackie's pillbox hat opened at once, and a swarm of bees flew out and swooped down on the veggies in Bumbly Park.

"Oh! A wall of *bees*," cried Herbert and Wally as they scurried back to the factory.

But not everyone was afraid. In fact, several veggies got out cans of high-powered bee repellent and continued on with their jogging and chess games.

"Do we get to croc 'em, now?" Jackie asked, dancing with delight.

"Yes, luv! Time to croc 'em!"

Outback pushed a button on a remote-control device, and a huge door opened on the side of the huge hat on top of the huge hot-air balloon. (Remember, the balloon looked just like Jackie.) Out dropped...

One crocodile.

Two crocodiles.

Three crocodiles.

Four. Five. Six. Seven.

With parachutes attached to their scaly backs, the crocodiles fell to earth like reptilian bombs. But these weren't ordinary crocs. They were *hungry* crocodiles. Mean crocs. For three straight days, they had been forced to listen to a CD of the Bumblyburg Yodeling Club, so they were looking for someone to bite.

Vegetable stew sounded good to them.

"AHHHHHHHHHHHHHHHHH!"

As the crocs hit the ground running, Veggies scattered in all directions, running out of the park as fast they could.

"Check, mate!" Outback shouted to the elderly guys who finally fled their chess game.

"AHHHHHHHHHHHHHHHHH!"

Outback's plan was running like clockwork.

CHAPTER 15

THE CROCS TAKE OVER

Larryboy was startled by the wall of fleeing veggies as he raced his Larrymobile toward the center of town.

"What's going on?" he called to three running scallions.

"Crocodiles have taken over Bumbly Park!" shouted one scallion. "Run for your life!"

Putting his foot to the floor, the Larrymobile shot forward. When Larryboy reached the park, he could see that an army of crocodiles had made a circle around the statue of Sir Lester Bumbly.

All the veggies had fled—except Ma Mushroom. She wasn't going to budge. She was determined to sit and eat her three-scoop ice cream cone in peace. When a crocodile came at her, Ma Mushroom gave it a blistering look. Knowing better, the croc retreated, whimpering like a scolded puppy.

Meanwhile, Outback Jack drifted down from the sky in his hot-air balloon. As you recall (you'll be tested on this), Outback's jeep dangled from the bottom of the balloon. But what you probably didn't know was that a mechanical digging device was attached to the front end.

"Be careful, Larryboy," Archie called out over the Larrymobile radio. "That giant Jackie balloon could be outfitted with dastardly secret weapons."

"I'm ready for any secret weapon he's got, Archie."

THWACK! THWACK! THWACK!

The Larrymobile fired three X-42 mega-plungers at the nearest crocodiles, allowing the superhero to slip past them.

"Good shot, Larryboy!" boomed a voice from somewhere above.

Glancing up over his shoulder, Larryboy was shocked to see Pruneman—flying! Evidently, Pruneman had finally mastered his Prune-Pit-Power-Up Move. Prune pits streamed out of the large down-turned ears on his costume mask, propelling him forward at incredible speed.

Larryboy had a sinking feeling. The last time Pruneman tried to help, he had messed up everything. Pruneman was just too old for this kind of thing.

Larryboy opened his cockpit and shouted, "You're flying? Isn't that a little dangerous at your age?"

"No problemo," grinned Pruneman. "Flying is like riding a bike. Once you learn, you never forget. Once you…**WHOOOOAAAAAAAAAA!"** Suddenly, Pruneman's stream of prune pits went berserk. The elderly superhero started to zig when he was supposed to zag.

"Come to think of it, I never did learn how to ride a bike!" Pruneman shouted as he roared out of control, skimming just two feet over Ma Mushroom's head.

"Whippersnapper!"

Larryboy quickly positioned the Larrymobile beneath Outback's hot-air balloon and fired a plunger, which arced upward about fifty feet. The plunger connected with the door of Outback's jeep.

THWACK!

Larryboy scrambled up the tether line, climbing all of the way up to the door of the jeep. There he found himself staring into the face of pure evil—Jackie the Sock Puppet!

"Cease your villainous..." Larryboy started to say.

"Oh, shove off!" scoffed Outback.

Outback Jack simply flung his door open and Larryboy, who was hanging on to the door, was flung back as well. He was smashed like a bug against the side of the jeep.

"OOOOFFF!"

"Are you all right, Larryboy?" called Archie over the plunger-com. "What happened?"

"I forgot the old 'car door' trick," Larryboy answered in a pinched voice.

Larryboy's plunger suddenly popped loose from the door. Then his eyes crossed as he slid down the side of the jeep and tumbled to earth.

Larryboy yelled: **"PRUNEMAN!"**

That was his last word before the purple, plunger-pelting hero plummeted. (Try saying that ten times really fast.)

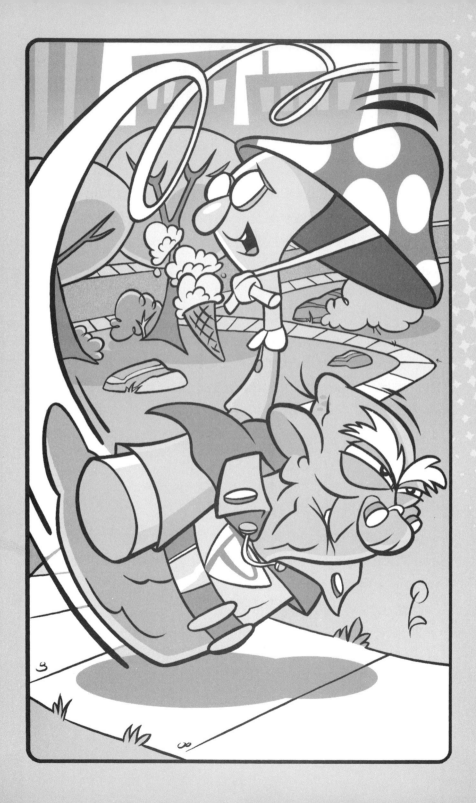

CHAPTER 16

UN-BEE-LIEVABLE!

Larryboy was fifty feet from the ground and falling fast.

"Don't fear, Larryboy! Help is on the way!" Pruneman shouted.

Only one problem. Pruneman was still having a hard time getting his Prune-Pit-Power-Up Move under control. He dipped. He barrel-rolled. He loop-de-looped. He nearly crashed a dozen times.

Larryboy was now forty-five feet from the ground.

At last, Pruneman got his target in sight. Weaving like a bird that had lost its flying permit, Pruneman swooped down and scooped up...

Ma Mushroom?

"Oops," said Pruneman.

"What's the big idea, whippersnapper!" shouted Ma Mushroom. She had been minding her own business, eating her three-scoop ice cream cone. Now she found herself scooped up, perched on Pruneman's back, taking the ride of her life.

"Sorry, Ma,"

said Pruneman. "I thought you were Larryboy."

"How could you mistake me for a hairy boy?" scowled Ma Mushroom. "You're just lucky my ice cream cone is still in one piece."

Ma Mushroom peered at Pruneman over the top of her glasses. "You've got prune pits coming out of your ears," she noted in disbelief. Then, as an afterthought, she said, "Pretty cool."

Meanwhile, Larryboy was now twenty feet from the ground. In a few more moments, he was going to be Pancake-Boy.

"WHOOOOOAAAA NELLIE!" yelled Ma Mushroom as Pruneman made a sharp turn, reversing direction. One of her ice cream scoops popped up in the air, but she caught it before it fell.

The out-of-control Pruneman roared through two back-yards, plucking a laundry line of clothes clear out of the ground. Then he bore right through a large quilt, creating a mushroom-shaped hole.

"I've got lint on my ice cream," Ma Mushroom complained. "Watch it, sonny!"

Just seconds before Larryboy hit the ground, Pruneman finally regained control of his prune-pit stream. But he still wasn't close enough to pluck Larryboy out of the air.

THWOPP! THWACK!

Just in time, Larryboy fired off a plunger, which attached itself to Ma Mushroom's face. The line held and Larryboy was pulled up, up into the air, and towed behind the flying Pruneman.

"Whippersnapper!" Ma Mushroom's muffled voice came from inside the plunger.

Larryboy was saved! That was the good news.

The bad news was that while all of this was happening, the hot-air balloon had landed and Outback Jack had gone digging. He had already ripped out the statue and was chewing into the soil.

"We gotta stop them!" Larryboy shouted, while being dragged across the sky.

"Don't worry, Larryboy, I'm on it," said Pruneman.

Carrying Ma Mushroom, dragging Larryboy, and trailing a laundry-line of clothes, Pruneman changed directions and raced straight for Outback.

"The old geezer and that purple guy are heading our way," said Jackie the Sock Puppet as Outback hurried to retrieve the treasure.

"Blimey, they don't give up, do they? Well—you know what must be done."

"Sure do," said Jackie.

Jackie poked a button on Outback's remote control. Then the lid opened on the huge pink hat that sat on top of the huge crocodile balloon. Out came the largest insect imaginable. It looked like a prehistoric bug.

It was a *giant* Mega Jester-Bee, and it was headed straight for our heroes!

CHAPTER 17

THE SANDS OF TIME

"Our awesome Aussie bee
will keep those blokes busy for awhile,"
explained Outback, tearing into the ground
with his digging device.

CLUNK!

"I think you've hit something, Jack!" said the sock puppet. "And it sounds like metal."

"That's the sound of a bloomin' treasure chest, luv! That's also the sound of us getting rich!"

Sure enough, the mechanical shovel dug deeply, lifting out two humongous chests. Then it dropped them to the ground, along with a load of dirt and sod.

"Me treasure!" Jackie sang out. "I'm going to buy a pony! I'm going to buy a pony!"

Leaping from his jeep, Outback grabbed a crowbar, stuck it into the treasure chest latch, and yanked. The chest cracked open like an oyster. Breathless, Outback threw back the lid. He couldn't believe he was about to become rich beyond his wildest dreams. He stepped back and feasted his eyes on the glorious wonders of...

Sand?

Outback lifted out a scoop of what was supposed to be gold. But it wasn't. The treasure chest was filled with beach sand. In a panic, Outback cracked open the second chest—and found more of the same. Sand, sand, sand!

He overturned the chests, hoping to find jewels buried beneath the sand. But there was nothing!

"We've been duped, luv!"

"I could have told you there'd be no treasure under that statue," said someone nearby.

Outback wheeled around and found himself staring at Pruneman, Larryboy, and Ma Mushroom. Our heroes were back on level ground, ready to make an arrest.

"I knew there was no treasure buried here in the park," repeated Pruneman.

"You did?" Larryboy asked, just as surprised as Outback.

"Yes. I tried to tell you back at the retirement home," Pruneman explained. "But you took off before I had a chance."

"My bad," said Larryboy.

"Isn't it time for your nap, Prunejuiceman?" Outback snarled at the old hero.

Larryboy's blood boiled. "You've got a lot of nerve calling him Prunejuiceman. Pruneman is a hero! He's been saving people since before you were born."

"He's an old coot."

"Rise in the presence of the aged, show respect for the elderly, and revere your God," Larryboy said, repeating the words from Bok Choy's class.

"What in the world are you blabbing about?" Outback scoffed.

"We should show respect to our elders," said Larryboy. "Respect! That's spelled 'R–E–S–P–E–C–T.'"

Suddenly, Jackie the Sock Puppet burst out in song. "R–E–S–P–E–C–T! Tell me what it means to me! R–E–S–P–E–C–T! Sock it to me, sock it to me, sock it to me, sock it..."

"Stuff a sock in it, Jackie!" Outback yelled.

"Sorry. I always get carried away by that song."

Outback turned his back on Larryboy, furious. "The only thing I'm going to show you and Pruneman is a good thrashing, mate. And when I'm done, I'm going to tear this city apart until I find that bloomin' treasure."

"And how do you plan to do that?" asked Pruneman.

(This is the part where the evil villain unwittingly gives away his plan.)

"After my Mega Jester-Bee sprays laughing gas on the entire city, no one will be able to stop me," laughed Outback. "I'll go house to house and building to building until I find that treasure! Blimey, you blokes just don't get it, do you?"

Larryboy turned and gazed toward downtown Bumblyburg. Sure enough, Outback's evil plan was already hatching.

The big bad bee dive-bombed the city, spraying its cloud of green gas like a crop duster. As the green gas settled on the city, hundreds of veggie citizens suddenly found themselves wearing gag glasses with silly attached noses and moustaches. Bad jokes would abound as Outback Jack buzzed through the city in search of the treasure.

It was no laughing matter.

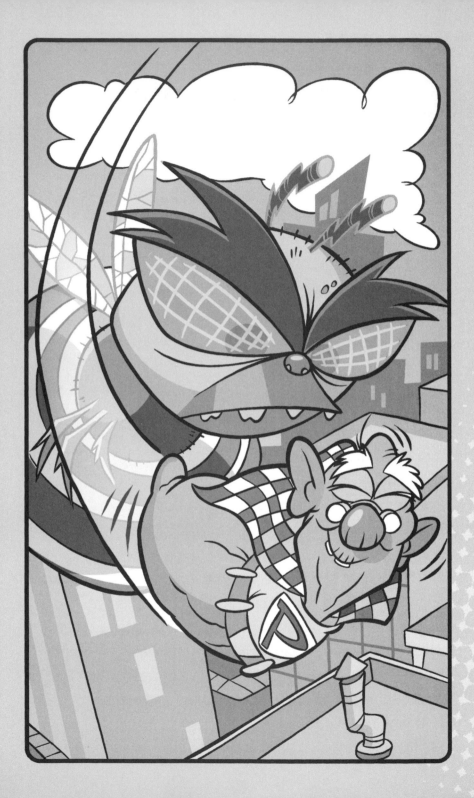

CHAPTER 18

POP! GOES THE WEASELS

Before Ma Mushroom
could even mutter, "whippersnapper,"
Pruneman, the elderly superhero raced to
the rescue. With his checkered tablecloth
cape flapping in the wind, he swooped down
on the giant bee, zipping within inches of the
creature's giant eyes.

The bee's attention was taken away from the
city—just for a moment.

Pruneman zipped by the big bee a second time.

By the third time, the monster was furious. The
senior superhero was pestering the giant bee in the
same way that bees pester veggies during sweet summer picnics.

Turning away from the city's downtown, the giant
bee took off after Pruneman.

"Say goodbye to the old coot, Larryboy," Outback
said as they watched the scene unfold from a distance. "That bloomin' bee is going to finish him
off! As for me, I'm heading into town to find me
some treasure. G'day, mate."

Outback hopped into his hot-air balloon

and prepared for takeoff. But if Outback had been a little wiser, he might have realized what Pruneman was trying to do. He wasn't just luring the bee away from Bumblyburg. He was luring the bee *toward* Outback.

Pruneman raced across the sky, with the bloated bee just several feet behind him. If it hadn't been for a couple of quick dodges, the monster might have had him. Instead, Pruneman zeroed in on the hot-air balloon, which was just beginning to rise from the ground.

SWOOOOOSHHHHH!
BUZZZZZZZZZZZZZ!

Pruneman and the bee cut a path right past Outback's balloon.

"Blimey, what was that?" Outback said, looking up.

"I don't like the looks of this," cried Jackie.

SWOOOOOSHHHHH!
BUZZZZZZZZZZZZZ!

"Oy, that was close!" Outback grumbled, getting a little nervous.

On the third pass, Pruneman shouted to Larryboy. "Use your plungers, Larryboy!"

Larryboy took aim. He fired.

THONK!

The plunger struck home, hitting the bee square in the forehead. With startling power, the force of the plunger sent the giant bee reeling backward, tumbling toward the hot-air balloon, stinger first.

POP!

The giant stinger sank deep into the balloon. Air

escaped so fast that the balloon whipped around with the big bee's stinger still lodged inside.

"Hang on, Jackie!" yelled Outback.

"**AHHHHHHHHH!**" screamed the sock puppet.

The punctured balloon shot off into the distance, zipping up and down, back and forth, and to and fro (wherever "fro" is). The balloon made the kind of wild moves that you might expect on one of the Ten-Rides-Most-Likely-to-Make-You-Wish-You-Hadn't-Eaten-a-Big-Breakfast.

When all the air had finally leaked out, the balloon crash-landed just feet from Officer Olaf and his paddy wagon.

Special delivery.

"I'm sorry I let you down, luv," said Outback Jack to his sock puppet as the officer tossed the villains into the paddy wagon. "I tried my best, but Prunejuiceman was sharper than I thought."

Jackie simply turned away in a huff. "Talk to the hand, Outback. Talk to the hand."

"Watch it, luv. You were just dirty laundry before I came along. I *made* you!"

Officer Olaf slammed the paddy wagon door closed with a deafening **CLANG!**

CHAPTER 19

THE GOLDEN YEARS

With Outback and Jackie behind bars, the city of Bumblyburg was safe and sound once again. Veggies poured out of their homes and offices, cheering Larryboy for what he had done. But Larryboy gave the credit to Pruneman.

"Pruneman?" asked many of the veggies. "Never heard of him. He must be some new superhero."

"He doesn't look new. Looks pretty ancient."

If only they knew...

Far into the night, the celebrations continued. In fact, Larryboy and Pruneman didn't even get a chance for some well-deserved rest until long after their bedtimes.

By the next day, Larryboy was feeling as good as new and was eager to visit Pruneman at the Home for Retired Superheroes. Only this time, he didn't have to be forced to go.

"We made a good team, didn't we?" said Larryboy, casting his eyes at the clocks in the Clock Room.

"We sure did," agreed Pruneman.

"But you know, it doesn't seem fair," said Larryboy.

"What doesn't seem fair?"

"Over your long life, you've rescued this city again and again, Pruneman. But people always forget. Even *I* forgot what you did for us so long ago. It shouldn't take something like this for people to remember—and respect you."

"Time passes," Pruneman said. "I try not to let it bother me."

"Show respect for the elderly and revere your God," Larryboy said to himself, trying not to forget the words from his *Superhero Handbook*. "By the way, if the Treasure of Bumblyburg wasn't under the statue of Sir Lester Bumbly, then where is it hidden?"

Pruneman grinned. "I'm sorry, Larryboy, but I promised I would keep it a secret. I'm afraid I cannot tell *even* you."

Larryboy shrugged good-naturedly. "That's OK. I wouldn't want you to break your promise. Say, how about a game of Superhero Bingo?"

"I'd love it."

As Larryboy bounced out of the Clock Room, Pruneman paused to glance around. His eyes fell on the hourglasses lining one of the walls, and he smiled.

Sand flowed from one end of the hourglasses to the other. But if someone had taken the time to look carefully, he or she would have noticed that the sand in the hourglasses flashed with glints of gold.

Time is golden. Time is truly a treasure from God. Just ask any senior superhero.

Pruneman closed the door to the Clock Room and hurried after Larryboy.

"WE ARE THOSE HEROES!" shouted the dynamic duo as they bounded into the multi-purpose room, side by side.

THE END

Larryboy and the Sinister Snow Day
Softcover 0-310-70561-4

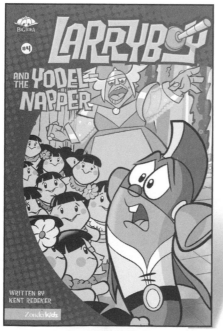

Larryboy and the Yodelnapper
Softcover 0-310-70562-2

Larryboy and the Angry Eyebrows
(Episode 1) VHS

Larryboy in … Leggo My Ego
(Episode 2) VHS

Larryboy in … The Yodelnapper
(Episode 3) VHS